HarperPerennial

A Division of HarperCollins*Publishers*

I Told You So, You Blockhead!

PEANUTS
TREASURY

Charles M. Schulz

HarperCollins books may be purchased for
educational, business, or sales promotional use.
For information please write to:
Special Markets Department, HarperCollins Publishers, Inc.,
10 East 53rd Street, New York, NY 10022

http://www.harpercollins.com

Designed by Christina Bliss, Staten Island

FIRST EDITION

ISBN 0-06-107562-0

Printed in U.S.A.

3

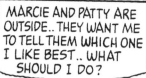

MARCIE AND PATTY ARE OUTSIDE.. THEY WANT ME TO TELL THEM WHICH ONE I LIKE BEST.. WHAT SHOULD I DO?

TELL 'EM YOU CAN'T STAND EITHER ONE OF THEM! TELL 'EM TO GET LOST! SIC YOUR DOG ON 'EM!

1-3-92

YOU'VE TAKEN TOO LONG TO DECIDE, CHUCK, SO WE'RE GOING HOME..

GO BACK TO SLEEP.. I WON'T NEED YOU..

DID THEY HAVE ANY COOKIES?

1-4-92

I MEAN, HOW CAN YOU TELL ONE PERSON YOU LIKE HER MORE THAN THE OTHER PERSON WITHOUT HURTING THAT PERSON'S FEELINGS?

IF IT WERE A MOUSE AND A CAT, I'D HAVE NO TROUBLE AT ALL!

4

"ALL RIGHT," SAID THE CAT, AND THIS TIME IT VANISHED QUITE SLOWLY BEGINNING WITH THE END OF THE TAIL...

..AND ENDING WITH THE GRIN

"IT'S THE MOST CURIOUS THING I EVER SAW," THOUGHT ALICE..

HERE, LET ME SEE WHAT YOU'RE READING..

"WOOF WOOF WOOF WOOF WOOF WOOF WOOF WOOF"

THAT'S RIDICULOUS!

THE LADY AT THE LIBRARY SAID HER DOG LOVED IT

6

8

11

16

"'ALL RIGHT,' SAID THE CAT; AND THIS TIME IT VANISHED QUITE SLOWLY...ENDING WITH THE GRIN WHICH REMAINED SOME TIME AFTER THE REST OF IT HAD GONE"

GRINS ARE EASY...

NOSES ARE HARDER..

I DON'T RECALL SAYING THAT YOU COULD SHARE THIS BLANKET...

BUT I GUESS ANIMALS HAVE RIGHTS, TOO, DON'T THEY?

FROM THE DAY THE WORLD BEGAN..

FORTY-THREE, AND NINE, AND TWENTY-SIX, AND THIRTEEN, AND FIFTY-SEVEN ...HMM....

1-31

YES, MA'AM..WELL, ALL I CAN SAY IS...

THEY SURE ADD UP, DON'T THEY?

© 1992 United Feature Syndicate, Inc.

"'ALL RIGHT,' SAID THE CAT, AND THIS TIME IT VANISHED QUITE SLOWLY"

© 1992 United Feature Syndicate, Inc.

"'WELL! I'VE OFTEN SEEN A CAT WITHOUT A GRIN,' THOUGHT ALICE; 'BUT A GRIN WITHOUT A CAT! IT'S THE MOST CURIOUS THING...'"

GRINS ARE EASY... NOSES ARE HARD...

EARS ARE ALMOST IMPOSSIBLE..

2-3

18

19

I THOUGHT I HEARD A SPLASH

I WONDER WHERE YOU GO TO GIVE UP THE GAME..

YES, MA'AM.."A TALE OF TWO CITIES"

CHARLIE DICKENS

CHUCK? CHAZ? CHARLES? WHATEVER..

THIS IS MY REPORT ON "A TALE OF TWO CITIES" BY CHARLES DICKENS..

" ST. PAUL AND MINNEAPOLIS ARE..."

ONE OF THE GREAT TRIES OF ALL TIME, SIR

26

28

RAINWATER FALLS FROM THE SKY AND BECOMES SWIMMING POOL WATER AND CAR WASHING WATER...

2-26

WITHOUT RAINWATER YOUR SWIMMING POOL WOULD BE EMPTY AND YOUR CAR WOULD BE DIRTY..

HAVING SAID ALL THAT, HERE IS A QUESTION FOR YOU...

© 1992 United Feature Syndicate, Inc.

HOW DID MY FOOT GET CAUGHT IN THIS STUPID PAIL ?!

I LOVED YOUR REPORT TODAY ON RAINWATER, SIR.. I HOPE THE TEACHER GAVE YOU A GOOD GRADE..

ANOTHER D-MINUS!

© 1992 United Feature Syndicate, Inc.

2-27

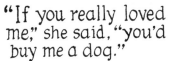

"If you really loved me," she said, "you'd buy me a dog."

3-2

So he bought her a dog.

It was not too long before the dog wished he had never become involved.

SO I SUPPOSE YOU HAVE TO ASK YOURSELF, "WHICH WOULD I RATHER HAVE HAPPEN..MY KITE GET CAUGHT IN A TREE OR RUN OVER BY A TRUCK?"

3-3 © 1992 United Feature Syndicate, Inc.

THEY SAY THAT A BALL DROPPED FROM WAIST HEIGHT WILL HIT THE GROUND AT A SPEED OF 9.45 MILES PER HOUR

SO?

3-6

SO, INSTEAD OF PITCHING IT, WHY DON'T YOU JUST DROP IT?

HEY, SWEETIE! YOU SURE LOOK CUTE TODAY!

SEXUAL HARASSMENT! SEXUAL HARASSMENT!

IT'S GOING TO BE A LONG SEASON..

3-7

HE'S LEAVING ME! I'M BEING ABANDONED! MY LIFE IS RUINED...

3-11

SO LONG, OLD FRIEND! WE'LL BE BACK IN A FEW DAYS..

COME ON, DOG.. LET'S GO INSIDE...

HERE'S THE WORLD WAR I FLYING ACE BEING LED OFF TO PRISONER OF WAR CAMP..

© 1992 United Feature Syndicate, Inc.

ALL RIGHT, IF YOU'RE GOING TO BE STAYING HERE FOR A FEW DAYS, I SHOULD KNOW YOUR FEEDING SCHEDULE...

© 1992 United Feature Syndicate, Inc.

I WONDER IF YOU PREFER EATING IN THE MORNING, AT NOON OR AT NIGHT...

3-12

SURE!

36

I SUPPOSE I SHOULD TELL YOU THIS RIGHT NOW... IN OUR HOUSE, ANIMALS ARE NOT ALLOWED ON THE COUCH...

SO YOU'LL HAVE TO GET OFF!

3-13

WHO, ME?

CHARLIE BROWN'S DOG SEEMS KIND OF SAD...

WELL, I SUPPOSE HE MISSES HIS OWNER..

3-14

MAYBE YOU COULD GIVE HIM A TOY TO PLAY WITH OR SOMETHING TO CHEER HIM UP...

37

I WONDER IF THAT ROUND-HEADED KID IS EVER GOING TO COME AND TAKE ME BACK HOME..

THEY SAY DOGS HAVE NO SENSE OF THE PASSING OF TIME...

I WONDER IF HE'S BEEN GONE FIVE MINUTES OR A HUNDRED YEARS..

I TOLD YOU THAT IN OUR HOUSE DOGS AREN'T ALLOWED ON THE FURNITURE!

I THINK IT'S BEEN A HUNDRED YEARS..

PERHAPS YOU DIDN'T UNDERSTAND.. CHARLIE BROWN ISN'T GOING TO BE GONE FOREVER, YOU KNOW...

ACTUALLY, YOU'RE ONLY GOING TO BE STAYING WITH US FOR A FEW DAYS..

SO YOU DON'T HAVE TO SEND OUT "CHANGE OF ADDRESS" CARDS..

AND ANOTHER THING..IN OUR HOUSE WE DON'T ALLOW DOGS TO BEG AT THE TABLE!

I'M NOT BEGGING.. I WAS JUST SITTING HERE, AND HAPPENED TO BE FACING YOUR WAY..

3-18

© 1992 United Feature Syndicate, Inc.

YOU DIDN'T EAT ALL OF YOUR DINNER SO I GUESS YOU DON'T GET ANY DESSERT..

3-19

?

© 1992 United Feature Syndicate, Inc.

AND YOU CAN'T ROAST MARSHMALLOWS IN THE BACK YARD AT TWO O'CLOCK IN THE MORNING!

PEANUTS

by SCHULZ

© 1992 United Feature Syndicate, Inc.

3-22

CLOMP

HA! THOUGHT YOU'D GET THIS BLANKET DIDN'T YOU? BUT I WAS TOO QUICK FOR YOU WASN'T I?

THIS IS MY REPORT ON THE TOOTH I LOST LAST NIGHT..

I JUST LEARNED THAT THE TOOTH FAIRY SENDS ALL THE TEETH SHE COLLECTS TO THE FACTORY WHERE THEY MAKE BILLIARD BALLS...

3-25

YOU MAY WANT TO CONSIDER THIS THE NEXT TIME YOU LEAVE A TOOTH UNDER YOUR PILLOW..

SCHULZ

SORRY TO WAKE YOU UP, BIG BROTHER, BUT I'VE BEEN THINKING...

I HAVE BEGUN TO DOUBT THE EXISTENCE OF THE TOOTH FAIRY..

IS IT WRONG TO LIE AWAKE AT NIGHT THINKING ABOUT SUCH THINGS?

ONLY IF YOU EXPECT AN ANSWER..

I'LL GO ASK YOUR DOG..

3-26

SCHULZ

YES, MA'AM.. MAY I HAVE PERMISSION TO GO HOME EARLY?

3-31

I SEE IT'S STARTING TO RAIN..

I THINK MY DOG IS GETTING WET..

YES, MA'AM.. I NEED TO RUN HOME BECAUSE IT'S RAINING, AND I'M AFRAID MY DOG IS GETTING WET...

YES, HE HAS A DOGHOUSE, BUT HE NEVER GOES IN IT...

NO, HE DOESN'T HAVE AN UMBRELLA..I DON'T KNOW WHAT HE DOES WHEN IT RAINS..

4-1

46

YOU SURE GOT YOURSELF WET SITTING OUT THERE IN THE RAIN, SNOOPY...

BUT AFTER I TOWEL YOU OFF, YOU'LL BE NICE AND WARM AND FUZZY...

I MAY HAVE TO GO INTO HIDING..

4-2

YES, MA'AM..MY DOG AND I WANT TO THANK YOU FOR ALLOWING ME TO GO HOME EARLY YESTERDAY BECAUSE HE WAS SITTING IN THE RAIN..

4-3

IN FACT, HE WOULD LIKE TO THANK YOU IN PERSON...

NO, THAT'S ALL RIGHT... WE UNDERSTAND..

WE DO?

52

56

"FOR LO, THE WINTER IS PAST..THE RAIN IS OVER AND GONE.."

4-27

"..THE VOICE OF THE TURTLEDOVE IS HEARD IN OUR LAND"

© 1992 United Feature Syndicate, Inc.

HURRY UP, AND PITCH, YOU BLOCKHEAD!

I DON'T THINK THAT WAS A TURTLEDOVE..

HOW COME WE RIDE A BUS TO SCHOOL?

© 1992 United Feature Syndicate, Inc.

WHY DON'T THEY HAUL US THERE IN A TRUCK..THEN DUMP US IN THE BACK WITH THE REST OF THE TRASH?

4-28

STILL HAVING TROUBLE WITH FRACTIONS, HUH?

BUS STOP

HOW CAN WE DO THIS IF THERE'S NO SNOW ON THE GROUND?

4-29

THE GRASS IS JUST AS GOOD..MAYBE EVEN BETTER..

ON THE OTHER HAND, THERE'S A LOT TO BE SAID FOR SNOW..

HERE'S THE WORLD WAR I FLYING ACE ACTING AS OBSERVER IN A TWO-SEATER..

4-30

I HAVE OBSERVED THAT I DON'T THINK I WANT TO DO THAT AGAIN..

Tears formed in his eyes as he read her letter of farewell.

"We will always have our memories," she wrote.

Suddenly, he realized it was a form letter.

5-7

WHAT DID SHE SAY?

SHE SAID, "THE FOLLOWING TEST WAS MADE POSSIBLE BY A GRANT FROM YOUR TEACHER"

IF YOU HAVE A PLEDGE BREAK, MA'AM, I'M LEAVING!

5-8

Panel 1: IF YOU STRIKE OUT THIS LAST GUY, CHARLIE BROWN, YOU'RE GOING TO MAKE HIM VERY VERY UNHAPPY..

Panel 2: THAT'S RIGHT.. ARE YOU SURE YOU WANT TO BRING UNEXPECTED GRIEF INTO THAT POOR KID'S LIFE?

Panel 3: JUST WHAT I NEED... NINTH-INNING ETHICS..

5-9

Panel 4: It was a dark and stormy night.

5-11

Panel 5: NO WONDER YOUR STORIES NEVER SELL...THEY ALL BEGIN THE SAME WAY..

Panel 6: It was a dark and stormy noon.

5-2

The Story of My Life

I come from a very poor family.

We were so poor we had to eat cat food. So we all died.

YOU ALL DIED?

WELL, NOT EXACTLY

5-12

BUT THE CAT WAS FURIOUS

DO YOU EVER HAVE ANY REGRETS?

ME?

5-13

I MEAN, I SUPPOSE WE ALL THINK ABOUT HOW WE..

ME?

I MEAN, WE SORT OF LOOK BACK, AND...

ME?

IT JUST SEEMS THAT..

ME?

YES, MA'AM, I WAS SICK FOR A COUPLE OF DAYS...HERE'S MY EXCUSE..

NO, MA'AM, NOTHING SERIOUS...

5-14

I THINK MAYBE I HAD THE FIFTY-THREE HOUR FLU..

THIS STUPID ERASER SMUDGES EVERYTHING!

PENCIL ERASERS ARE SPOILED BY EXPOSURE TO ULTRAVIOLET LIGHT OR OZONE IN THE AIR, SIR..

AN ERASER CAN EVEN BE SPOILED BY LEAVING IT ON A WINDOWSILL..

THERE'S MY PROBLEM, MA'AM..MY HEAD IS SPOILED FROM SITTING TOO CLOSE TO THE WINDOWSILL..

5-15

© 1992 United Feature Syndicate, Inc.

66

TRUE! FALSE! TRUE! FALSE!

THIS ISN'T A "TRUE OR FALSE" TEST, SIR... IT'S MULTIPLE CHOICE..

IT'S TOO LATE NOW..

5-19

TRUE! FALSE! TRUE! FALSE!

ANYBODY HOME?

NO, I REALIZE YOU'RE NOT JUST ANYBODY..

5-20

PEANUTS by SCHULZ

IT'S A KNOWN FACT THAT DOGS ARE MORE ATHLETIC THAN BIRDS..

MOST BIRDS

5-23

YES, MA'AM..I GUESS I SHOULD HAVE USED A SHARPER PENCIL...

YES, MA'AM..WE EVEN HAVE AN ELECTRIC PENCIL SHARPENER AT HOME..

NO, MA'AM, I COULDN'T USE IT THIS MORNING...

I DIDN'T WANT TO WAKE UP MY DOG..

5-25

Panel 1: I'M LOOKING FORWARD TO A GOOD REPORT CARD NEXT WEEK.. LOOK AT THESE TEST PAPERS...

Panel 2: THE WAY I SEE IT, SEVEN "D-MINUSES" AVERAGE OUT TO AN "A"

5-28

Panel 3: SIMPLE ARITHMETIC, HUH, SIR? — YOU GOT IT, MARCIE

Panel 4: I'M DEPRESSED BECAUSE I DON'T WANT TO GO TO SUMMER CAMP THIS YEAR..

Panel 5: "SHE WAS PREY TO THE BROODING BROUGHT ON BY IRREVOCABLE PARTINGS"

Panel 6: THAT'S FROM "MADAME BOVARY" — 5/29

Panel 7: I SHOULD GIVE HER A CALL..

74

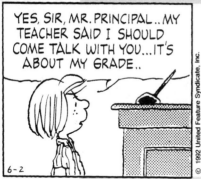

IF I WERE TO HIDE UNDER MY BED ALL SUMMER, I WOULDN'T HAVE TO GO TO CAMP, WOULD I?

THAT'S A GOOD IDEA..NO ONE WOULD KNOW WHERE YOU WERE..IT'S A PERFECT PLAN..

© 1992 United Feature Syndicate, Inc.

6-4

I'LL TRY TO THINK OF SOMETHING ELSE..

6-5

SO, BECAUSE YOU'RE A DOG, I GUESS YOU HAVE TO DEPEND ON ME, BUT I DON'T REALLY WANT YOU TO FEEL YOU HAVE TO DEPEND ON ME... YOU KNOW WHAT I'M SAYING?

WHY DO THEY ALWAYS HAVE TO SAY, "YOU KNOW WHAT I'M SAYING?"

© 1992 United Feature Syndicate, Inc.

77

LET'S GO TO THE DOUGHNUT SHOP..

WHAT A COINCIDENCE! I KNEW I HEARD A DOUGHNUT CALLING ME!

I HOPE THE SHOP ISN'T CLOSED..

DOUGHNUTS NEVER CALL FROM BEHIND LOCKED DOORS..

6-6

© 1992 United Feature Syndicate, Inc.

I'VE DECIDED I AM DEFINITELY NOT GOING TO SUMMER CAMP!

INSTEAD, I'M GOING TO HOLLYWOOD! IT'S MORE MY STYLE..

I HAVE TO LEAVE NOW..I'M FLYING ON "ACE" AIRLINES..

"ACE" AIRLINES?

© 1992 United Feature Syndicate, Inc.

6-8

IS THIS THE FLIGHT TO HOLLYWOOD?

YOU MUST BE THE BAGGAGE HANDLER, RIGHT?

6-9

DO I GET A CLAIM CHECK?

THE CLAIM CHECK IS BIGGER THAN THE BAGGAGE HANDLER..

WHAT KIND OF AN AIRLINE IS THIS? WHERE'S THE COMPLIMENTARY ORANGE JUICE?

AND ISN'T ANYONE GOING TO WELCOME ME ABOARD?

6-10

SMAK!

I'D RATHER HAVE THE ORANGE JUICE..

80

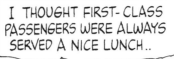

IT'S RAINING!

HEY, PILOT, CAN WE FLY IN THE RAIN?

6-16

PILOT?

© 1992 United Feature Syndicate, Inc.

WE WERE SUPPOSED TO BE FLYING TO HOLLYWOOD!

THEN IT STARTED TO RAIN, AND THE PILOT JUMPED OUT, AND I WAS IN MY OWN BACK YARD!

© 1992 United Feature Syndicate, Inc.

WHERE'S THAT PILOT?! I'M GONNA POUND HIM!!

AH! BONJOUR, MADEMOISELLE! I AM THE FAMOUS SERGEANT OF THE FOREIGN LEGION...

6-17

HEY! WHERE'RE YOU GOING WITH MY DOG?

THIS IS THE STUPID PILOT WHO LEFT ME IN THE RAIN!

AU CONTRAIRE! I AM THE FAMOUS SERGEANT OF THE FOREIGN LEGION!

6-18

JE TROUVE PARIS TRÈS BEAU! I THINK PARIS IS VERY BEAUTIFUL!

THERE! STAND OUT IN THE RAIN LIKE I HAD TO WHEN YOU LEFT ME SITTING ON YOUR STUPID PLANE!

I HOPE YOU AND YOUR PLANE GET SOAKING WET!

PLANE? I THOUGHT THIS WAS FORT ZINDERNEUF..

6-19

83

STRIKE THIS GUY OUT, CEMENT HEAD! YOU CAN DO IT, MUD HEAD!

WHICH TEAM ARE YOU YELLING FOR?

I DON'T KNOW.. WHICH TEAM AM I ON?

My life has been one of constant struggle

THAT'S A LAUGH

Ha Ha Ha Ha!

WHEN CAN WE GO HOME? IT'S BORING OUT HERE!

IT WOULDN'T BE BORING IF YOU'D CATCH THE BALL NOW AND THEN!

OH, SURE.. GET PERSONAL, HUH?

7-3

It was a dark and stormy night.

Suddenly, twenty-one shots rang out!

TWENTY-ONE SHOTS?

7-6

It was a twenty-one gun salute.

© 1992 United Feature Syndicate, Inc.

THIS IS THE LATEST FAD...I SAW THEM DOING IT IN TOWN...

7-7

"VELCRO" JUMPING! OUCH! OOOO!

I'VE DEVELOPED ANOTHER NEW PHILOSOPHY..REMEMBER, IT USED TO BE, "WHO CARES?"

NOW, IT'S, "WHAT DO I CARE?"

WELL, I'M VERY HAPPY FOR YOU

WHAT DO I CARE?

7/8

WE WERE SUPPOSED TO PLAY BALL TODAY, BUT IT LOOKS LIKE IT MAY RAIN..

WHAT DO I CARE?

7-9

THAT'S MY NEW PHILOSOPHY TO CARRY ME THROUGH LIFE.. "WHAT DO I CARE?"

IT MAY CARRY YOU RIGHT OUT THE BACK DOOR!

LOOK..IT'S A SAND CASTLE.. I MADE IT WITH MY BARE HANDS!

WHAT DO I CARE? THAT'S MY NEW PHILOSOPHY..

7-10

..WHICH MAY TAKE A WHILE TO BE ACCEPTED!

91

PEANUTS®

by Schulz

95

SWIMMING LESSONS TODAY, SIR.. WE'RE SUPPOSED TO BE ASSIGNED PARTNERS...

THE BUDDY SYSTEM, HUH? I WONDER WHO MY PARTNER IS...

7-16

HI, MISTER BROWN... MY NAME IS CORMAC..I'M YOUR SWIMMING BUDDY..

7-17

I ADMIT I DON'T KNOW MUCH ABOUT SWIMMING...

IS YOUR NOSE SUPPOSED TO GO ABOVE THE WATER OR BELOW THE WATER?

96

HI, MY NAME IS CORMAC.. I HAD MY FIRST SWIMMING LESSON THIS MORNING..

IF YOU'RE EVER DROWNING, DON'T BE AFRAID TO CALL ME

IN THE MEANTIME, WILL YOU HELP ME WITH THIS INNER TUBE? I CAN'T GET IT OVER MY HEAD..

7-18

WHAT DID YOU LEARN IN CAMP TODAY, CORMAC?

I LEARNED HOW TO READ A COMPASS

SEE? IF I FOLLOW THE NEEDLE, I CAN FIND MY WAY ANYWHERE IN THE WORLD!

EXCEPT IN THE BUSHES...WHERE AM I?

7-20

97

SEE THAT STAR, CORMAC? THAT'S THE NORTH STAR.. HERE'S YOUR CHANCE TO TRY OUT YOUR COMPASS

SEE IF THE NEEDLE ON YOUR COMPASS POINTS IN THE SAME DIRECTION AS THE NORTH STAR..

7-21

IT'LL NEVER WORK

WHY NOT?

I JUST DROPPED IT IN THE LAKE!

I THINK YOU'RE VERY BEAUTIFUL, MISS MARCIE.. WHEN YOU GROW UP, YOU SHOULD BE A MODEL..

THANK YOU, CORMAC..WHAT ARE YOU GOING TO BE WHEN YOU GROW UP?

7-22
SMOOTH!

98

SWIMMING LESSONS START IN FIVE MINUTES, SIR..

I'M GLAD WE'RE USING THE BUDDY SYSTEM.. I FEEL A LOT SAFER...

SURE.. I'M DROWNING, AND MY BUDDY IS EATING COOKIES!

7-23

WE'RE SUPPOSED TO WRITE HOME TO OUR PARENTS, CORMAC, AND TELL THEM WHAT A GREAT TIME WE'RE HAVING HERE AT CAMP..

EVEN IF WE'RE NOT? ISN'T THAT A LIE?

WELL, IT'S SORT OF A WHITE LIE..

LIES COME IN COLORS?

7-24

101

THE WATER SEEMS SORT OF WARM TODAY..

IT'S ALMOST TOO WARM, ISN'T IT?

7-25

NO, CORMAC..BLOWING WON'T COOL IT OFF..

WELL, SO LONG, CORMAC... I'M GOING HOME TODAY..

MAYBE WE'LL SEE EACH OTHER AGAIN SOMETIME..

7-27

AND IF YOU EVER NEED AN ATTORNEY, HERE'S MY CARD..

WELL, I'M BACK!

BACK FROM WHERE?

HAVE YOU BEEN AWAY? WHO ARE YOU? WHY TELL ME? WHAT TOOK YOU SO LONG?

IS THAT ALL YOU HAVE TO SAY?

DID YOU BRING ME ANYTHING?

7/28

HAVE YOU REALLY BEEN AWAY AT CAMP?

THEN I GUESS I SHOULD TAKE ALL MY THINGS OUT OF YOUR ROOM..

EVERY TIME I GO AWAY SOMEPLACE YOU MOVE INTO MY ROOM!

7-29

IT'LL TAKE TIME TO CHANGE THE LOCKS..

© 1992 United Feature Syndicate, Inc.

103

HOW WOULD YOU LIKE A NICE COLD GLASS OF WATER?

I'D LIKE IT VERY MUCH, THANK YOU..

8-1

DID I SAY "GLASS"? I MEANT "BUCKET"

I'LL THROW THE BALL, SEE?

THEN YOU GO BOUNDING AFTER IT, AND BRING IT BACK!

8-3

MAYBE WE SHOULD THINK ABOUT THIS A LITTLE MORE..

HERE'S HOW IT'S SUPPOSED TO WORK.. THE BALL IS THROWN, SEE...

WHEN YOU CHASE IT, YOU RUN WITH TOTAL ABANDON.. YOUR EARS ARE FLAPPING AND YOUR TONGUE IS FLYING!

THEN YOU BRING IT BACK WITH WILD ENTHUSIASM!

8-4

I DIDN'T SEE ANY EARS FLAP..

© 1992 United Feature Syndicate, Inc.

8-5

WELL, YES..THAT'S KIND OF WHAT I MEANT..

© 1992 United Feature Syndicate, Inc.

8-6

© 1992 United Feature Syndicate, Inc.

8-7

YOUR DOG ISN'T MUCH FOR CHASING A BALL, IS HE? OR MAYBE I JUST DON'T KNOW THE RIGHT WORD..

TRY "COOKIE"

BINGO!

© 1992 United Feature Syndicate, Inc.

OKAY! CHASE THE BALL, BRING IT BACK, AND I'LL GIVE YOU A COOKIE!

8-8

WHAT KIND OF COOKIE?

WHAT'S THIS? A BILL FOR A HUNDRED DOLLARS?

IT'S FROM "ACE AIRLINES". THEY SAY YOU NEVER PAID FOR YOUR TICKET...

8-10

I NEVER GOT WHERE I WAS GOING, EITHER! I NEVER GOT OUT OF OUR BACK YARD!

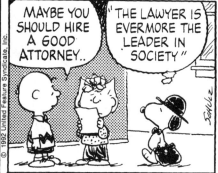

MAYBE YOU SHOULD HIRE A GOOD ATTORNEY..

"THE LAWYER IS EVERMORE THE LEADER IN SOCIETY"

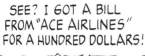

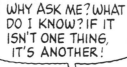

Panel 1: PARDON ME..DO YOU KNOW WHERE THE COURTHOUSE IS?

Panel 2: HOW SHOULD I KNOW? I'M JUST A LITTLE KID! I DON'T KNOW WHERE ANYTHING IS!

8-13

Panel 3: WHY ASK ME? WHAT DO I KNOW? IF IT ISN'T ONE THING, IT'S ANOTHER!

© 1992 United Feature Syndicate, Inc.

Panel 4: WELL, THANK YOU ANYWAY — HEY, NO PROBLEM

Panel 5: HOW CAN WE FIND THE COURTHOUSE IF WE DON'T KNOW WHAT A COURTHOUSE LOOKS LIKE?

Panel 6: IT'S PROBABLY A BIG BUILDING WITH LOTS OF PEOPLE STANDING AROUND..

8-14

© 1992 United Feature Syndicate, Inc.

Panel 7: I HOPE YOU'RE NOT IN A HURRY TO GET BACK HOME..

Panel 8: NOT REALLY.. I'VE ALREADY MISSED THE FIRST WEEK OF ATTORNEY CAMP..

111

SPIKE WAS NEVER ONE TO SIT HOME BY HIMSELF ON A SATURDAY NIGHT..

8-22

HELLO, CHARLIE BROWN? I'M SCARED..

OF WHAT? IT'S TWO O'CLOCK IN THE MORNING

I WAS SOUND ASLEEP.. AND THEN I HEARD SOME COYOTES HOWLING...

THEY SOUNDED SO LONELY.. I STARTED TO THINK ABOUT EVERYTHING IN THE WORLD, AND I GOT SCARED

I GUESS I WOKE YOU UP, HUH? WERE YOU ASLEEP?

NO, I WAS JUST SITTING HERE WAITING FOR SANTA CLAUS..

8-24

114

I'M SORRY I WOKE YOU UP LAST NIGHT, CHARLIE BROWN

WHEN I HEARD THOSE COYOTES HOWLING, THEY SOUNDED SO LONELY, I..

LINUS, THERE AREN'T ANY COYOTES WHERE WE LIVE..

8-25

I HEARD COYOTES HOWLING, CHARLIE BROWN

MAYBE IT WAS YOUR SISTER SNORING

DID SOMEBODY SAY, "SISTER"?

THERE! I HEAR THEM! I HEAR THE COYOTES HOWLING...

CHARLIE BROWN! I HEARD THE COYOTES AGAIN! THEY SOUNDED SO LONELY IT SCARED ME...

OH, I'M SORRY.. DID I WAKE YOU UP? IS THERE A TIME CHANGE WHERE YOU LIVE?

I DON'T THINK SO.. WE ONLY LIVE HALF A BLOCK APART..

8-26

115

WHEN I HEAR THOSE COYOTES HOWLING AT NIGHT, IT TOTALLY DEPRESSES ME..

I START TO FEEL LONELY...THEN I GET SCARED...

I THOUGHT HOLDING ONTO THAT BLANKET MADE YOU SECURE..

I THINK THE WARRANTY HAS RUN OUT..

8-27

THERE THEY GO AGAIN.. I CAN HEAR THOSE COYOTES HOWLING

8-28

HELLO, CHARLIE BROWN?

NO, THIS IS SALLY.. IS THIS MY SWEET BABBOO? HAVE YOU CALLED TO ASK ME TO GO TO THE MOVIES?

STUPID COYOTES!

SEE? THE SAME THING HAPPENED TO LEO TOLSTOY THAT'S BEEN HAPPENING TO YOU...

IT SAYS HE WOKE UP AT TWO O'CLOCK IN THE MORNING, AND HE WAS TERRIFIED!! "WHERE AM I?" HE ASKED HIMSELF.. "WHAT AM I RUNNING AWAY FROM?"

8-29

I'VE ALWAYS FELT THAT TOLSTOY AND I HAD SOMETHING IN COMMON..

GUESS WHAT, CHARLIE BROWN.. I HAVEN'T HEARD THE COYOTES HOWLING FOR TWO DAYS..

MAYBE THEY KNEW IT WAS BOTHERING YOU

HOW WOULD A BUNCH OF COYOTES KNOW THAT THEIR NIGHTTIME HOWLING WAS DEPRESSING ME?

I EXPLAINED IT TO THEM..

8-31

117

HERE'S THE WORLD WAR I FLYING ACE LEAPING FROM HIS BURNING PLANE

AS HE LANDS, HE SPRAWLS IN THE WET MUD..

SEVERELY WOUNDED, HE MUST MAKE HIS WAY BACK THROUGH ENEMY LINES...

HE MUST FIND AN AID STATION BEFORE HE COLLAPSES!

YPRES

THERE IT IS! THE ESSEX FARM DRESSING STATION!

AH! A BEAUTIFUL NURSE APPROACHES..

© 1992 United Feature Syndicate, Inc.

8-30

TRIPPED OVER YOUR SUPPER DISH AGAIN, I SEE..

SCHULZ

120

IF I STAND HERE, I CAN SEE THE LITTLE RED HAIRED GIRL WHEN SHE COMES OUT OF HER HOUSE...

9-3

OF COURSE, IF SHE SEES ME PEEKING AROUND THIS TREE, SHE'LL THINK I'M THE DUMBEST PERSON IN THE WORLD..

BUT IF I DON'T PEEK AROUND THE TREE, I'LL NEVER SEE HER...

WHICH MEANS I PROBABLY AM THE DUMBEST PERSON IN THE WORLD

WHICH EXPLAINS WHY I'M STANDING IN A BATCH OF POISON OAK..

I WASN'T CRITICIZING YOUR SWING...I JUST SAID I'VE NEVER SEEN A DIVOT LIKE THIS BEFORE..

9-4

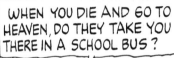

WHEN YOU DIE AND GO TO HEAVEN, DO THEY TAKE YOU THERE IN A SCHOOL BUS?

NO, THEY PICK YOU UP IN A GOLDEN CHARIOT..

SILVER, IF YOU COME IN SECOND

9-8

YES, MA'AM... THIS IS MY REPORT..

EACH MORNING I'D WAKE UP MY DOG, AND MAKE HIM HIS BREAKFAST..

THEN, I'D TAKE HIM FOR A WALK, AND MAKE HIS LUNCH..

AFTER HIS NAP, I'D FIX HIS SUPPER.. THIS IS WHAT I DID EVERY DAY..

YES, MA'AM? THE TITLE OF MY REPORT?

"HOW I SPENT MY SUMMER VACATION"

9-9

PSYCHIATRIC HELP 474

THE DOCTOR IS [IN]

WELL, I APPRECIATE THE HELP YOU'VE GIVEN ME

9-10

I WAS WONDERING, THOUGH, IF I SHOULD GET A SECOND OPINION..

ONLY IF YOU DON'T MIND MY BEATING YOU OVER THE HEAD WITH THAT STOOL YOU'RE SITTING ON!

THE DOCTOR IS [IN]

I GUESS FIRST OPINIONS ARE PRETTY GOOD..

YES, MA'AM.. AN AUTHENTIC REPORT ON OUR CONSTITUTION WRITTEN WITH AN AUTHENTIC FEATHER PEN...

9-11

AND A FEW AUTHENTIC SMUDGES..

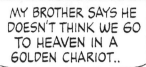 MY BROTHER SAYS HE DOESN'T THINK WE GO TO HEAVEN IN A GOLDEN CHARIOT..

 "OH, FOOLISH GALATIANS, WHO HATH BEWITCHED YOU?"

 9-15

 WHAT DOES "HATH" MEAN?

9-16

 YOU LIKE SPRING BETTER THAN FALL?

 WELL, YES... I CAN UNDERSTAND THAT..

128

THE BUS TO THE OBEDIENCE SCHOOL HAD AN ACCIDENT..

GOOD GRIEF! WAS ANYONE HURT?

WHAT ABOUT MY DOG? IS HE ALL RIGHT?

SOMEBODY SAID HE WAS THE HERO..

I'M HANDLING ALL THE LAWSUITS..

9-25

© 1992 United Feature Syndicate, Inc.

I HEAR THE JUDGE THREW YOUR CASE OUT OF COURT..

NO, HE SAID DOGS WEREN'T ALLOWED IN THE COURTROOM..

MY CASE GOT IN, BUT I DIDN'T

9-26

© 1992 United Feature Syndicate, Inc.

130

133

> I PLAN TO GROW..

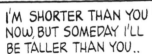

> I'M SHORTER THAN YOU NOW, BUT SOMEDAY I'LL BE TALLER THAN YOU..

> I'LL BE REAL TALL, AND YOU'LL HAVE TO LOOK STRAIGHT UP TO SEE MY EYES!

> IF A PERSON HAS A NICE SMILE, CORMAC, NOTHING ELSE MATTERS..

> I'LL HAVE A NICE SMILE AND VERY TALL TEETH!

137

"SHOW AN EXAMPLE OF THE SUBJUNCTIVE IN 'IF' CLAUSES FOR CONDITIONS CONTRARY TO FACT"

SORRY, MA'AM..I FORGOT TO FASTEN MY SEAT BELT..

10-13

I SAW A DOG ON TV DOING ALL SORTS OF TRICKS WITH HIS WATER DISH...

10-14

..AFTER HE EMPTIED THE WATER OUT

139

142

145

146

Panel 1:
LINUS, IF YOU'RE GOING TO TELL PEOPLE ABOUT THE "GREAT GRAPE," YOU'LL NEED HELP..

PUMPKIN

Panel 2:
WHATEVER.. ANYWAY, I'M VOLUNTEERING TO HELP YOU SPREAD THE WORD!

10-27

Panel 3:
ON HALLOWEEN NIGHT, THE "GREAT GRAPE" RISES OUT OF THE GRAPE PATCH, AND...

GOOD GRIEF!

SCHULZ

Panel 4:
THESE ARE PAMPHLETS ABOUT THE "GREAT PUMPKIN"...

Panel 5:
AND YOU WANT ME TO GO FROM DOOR TO DOOR AND GIVE THEM TO PEOPLE?

10-28

Panel 6:
ARE YOU COMING WITH ME?

I'LL BE RIGHT BEHIND YOU..

Panel 7:
GOOD AFTERNOON, MA'AM..I'D LIKE TO GIVE YOU THIS PAMPHLET ABOUT THE "GREAT GRAPE"

PUMPKIN!

SCHULZ

147

148

149

I HATE FIELD TRIPS... I'M ALWAYS SURE SOMETHING BAD IS GOING TO HAPPEN..

PSALM 121: VERSE 6 - "THE SUN SHALL NOT SMITE THEE BY DAY, NOR THE MOON BY NIGHT"

11-9

SOMEHOW, I'VE NEVER WORRIED MUCH ABOUT THE MOON..

THIS IS MY REPORT ON THE FIELD TRIP WE WENT ON YESTERDAY..

I DIDN'T GET SICK ON THE BUS

11-10

WE SHOULD GO ON MORE FIELD TRIPS..

LIKE MAYBE ONCE EVERY TEN YEARS..

AH, IT MUST BE VETERANS DAY..

I SEE THE FLYING ACE IS ON HIS WAY TO BILL MAULDIN'S HOUSE TO QUAFF A FEW ROOT BEERS

BILL MAULDIN WAS THE GREATEST CARTOONIST OF WORLD WAR II..

11-11

HE DREW GREAT MUD..

SEE THAT SKY? THAT SKY IS YOURS!

YOU'RE A BIRD! SOAR AS HIGH AS YOU WANT!

YOU CAN OWN THE SKY..

SORT OF..

11-12

RERUN, I HEAR YOU'RE GETTING PRETTY GOOD WITH YOUR NUMBERS..

LET'S HAVE A LITTLE TEST.. TELL ME WHAT YOU SEE...

FINGERS!

11-16

SO HERE I AM ON THE BACK OF MOM'S BICYCLE ON THE WAY TO THE GROCERY STORE..

PEDAL HARD, MOM! HARDER! THAT'S THE WAY!

11-17

LOOK OUT FOR THE LAWN MOWER!

GOOD! WE'RE OUT OF THE GARAGE!

155

SO HERE I AM RIDING ON THE BACK OF MY MOM'S BICYCLE..

NOW, WE TURN AROUND BECAUSE SHE FORGOT THE CAR KEYS...

NOW, SHE REMEMBERS SHE DOESN'T NEED THE CAR KEYS BECAUSE SHE'S RIDING HER BICYCLE..

11-18

MOM IS REALLY STRESSED OUT..

PEDAL FASTER, MOM! FASTER!

NO! SLOW DOWN! LOOK OUT FOR THE...

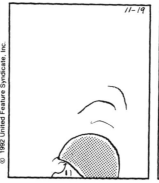
11-19

..POTHOLE!

© 1992 United Feature Syndicate, Inc.

156

SO I'M IN THE GROCERY STORE WITH MY MOM...

THIS LADY ASKS ME HOW OLD I AM... I TELL HER I'M A HUNDRED AND FIFTY..

EVERY TIME I RIDE ON THE BACK OF MY MOM'S BICYCLE, I AGE TWENTY YEARS!

11-20 © 1992 United Feature Syndicate, Inc.

OKAY, RERUN, LET'S WORK ON OUR COUNTING AGAIN..

NOW, HOW MANY FINGERS DO YOU SEE?

ALL BUT THE THUMB..

11-21 © 1992 United Feature Syndicate, Inc.

THEN, GUESS WHAT HAPPENED..

ABRAHAM TURNED AROUND, AND SAW THIS POOR RAM..

IT HAD ITS HORNS CAUGHT IN A THICKET..DID HE SET IT FREE? OF COURSE NOT!

© 1992 United Feature Syndicate, Inc.

HE OFFERED IT UP AS A BURNT OFFERING! CAN YOU IMAGINE THAT?! HE KILLED IT!!

HEY, SNOOPY, WE'RE INVITED OVER TO GRAMMA'S HOUSE FOR THANKSGIVING DINNER..

11-22

AND YOU KNOW WHAT THEY'RE GOING TO EAT? A BIRD!!

BLEAH!

HE'S NOT COMING ALONG?

DON'T ASK ME WHY.. I NEVER KNOW WHAT HE'S THINKING..

SCHULZ

11-23

11-24

CLOMP!

SOMETIMES I LIE AWAKE AT NIGHT, AND I ASK MYSELF...

..WHY ME?!

© 1992 United Feature Syndicate, Inc.

I'LL KNOW THE ANSWER!
I'LL KNOW THE ANSWER!

NO, NOT TODAY..
NOT TOMORROW..
NOT NEXT WEEK..

..BUT SOMEDAY
FOR SURE!

SMILE, MA'AM..YOU
LOOK NICE WHEN
YOU SMILE..

MA'AM?

IS THERE ANYTHING I CAN DO TO EARN A LITTLE EXTRA CREDIT?

12-7

SHOVEL YOUR WALK?

© 1992 United Feature Syndicate, Inc.

DID BEETHOVEN EVER PLAY "JINGLE BELLS"?

12-8

HE PROBABLY THOUGHT HE WAS TOO GOOD TO PLAY "JINGLE BELLS"

© 1992 United Feature Syndicate, Inc.

BONK!

IF I HAD BEEN THERE, I WOULD HAVE SAID, "HEY, LUDWIG, PLAY 'JINGLE BELLS'!"

LOOK WHAT MOM PUT IN MY LUNCH FOR US... CHRISTMAS COOKIES!

WOW! A WHOLE BUNCH! TOO BAD WE DON'T HAVE SOMEONE TO SHARE THEM...

12-10

12-17

HERE'S AN INTERESTING ITEM FROM NEEDLES, CALIFORNIA...

SOMEONE SNEAKED INTO THE CHAMBER OF COMMERCE BUILDING LAST NIGHT, AND PLUGGED IN AN EXTENSION CORD

THE CORD LED OUT OF TOWN SOMEWHERE INTO THE DESERT..

EVERYONE IS PUZZLED AS TO WHO OR WHY SOMEONE SHOULD DO SUCH A THING..

12-18

PEANUTS by Schulz

I SHOULD HAVE KNOWN!

SHOULD HAVE KNOWN WHAT?

172

HERE'S THE WORLD WAR I FLYING ACE SITTING IN A SMALL FRENCH CAFE.. IT IS CHRISTMAS EVE, AND HE IS DEPRESSED...

12-24

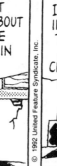

..BUT I SHOULDN'T COMPLAIN..WHAT ABOUT MY BROTHER SPIKE WHO'S OUT THERE IN THE TRENCHES?

I WONDER IF SPIKE IS THINKING ABOUT CHRISTMAS..

SCHULZ

12-25

SCHULZ

175